JULIETTE LOW

GIRL SCOUT FOUNDER

Written by
Helen Boyd Higgins

Illustrated by
Cathy Morrison

Patria Press, Inc.
3842 Wolf Creek Circle
Carmel, IN 46033
Phone 877–736–7930
Website: www.patriapress.com

Printed and bound in the United States of America

10 9 8 7 6 5 4 3 2 1

Text originally published by the Bobbs-Merrill Company, 1951 in the Childhood
of Famous Americans Series.® The Childhood of Famous Americans Series® is a
registered trademark of Simon & Schuster, Inc.

Patria Press and Young Patriots are trademarks of Patria Press, Inc. Other
product and company names mentioned herein may be the trademarks of their
respective owners. Use of any such marks herein does not imply association or
endorsement

Library of Congress Cataloging-in-Publication Data

Higgins, Helen Boyd.
    Juliette Low, Girl Scout founder / Helen Boyd Higgins ; illustrated by
Cathy Morrison.
        p. cm.— (Young patriots series ; 4)
Summary: Provides a fictional account of the childhood of the woman
responsible for the founding of the Girl Scouts of America.
    ISBN 1-882859-08-1 (hardcover)—ISBN 1-882859-09-X (pbk.)
    1. Low, Juliette Gordon, 1860-1927—Childhood and youth—Juvenile
fiction. [1. Low, Juliette Gordon, 1860-1927—Childhood and
youth—Fiction.] I. Morrison, Cathy, ill. II. Title. III. Series.
    PZ7.H53495 Ju 2002
    [Fic]—dc21   2001005463

Edited by Harold Underdown
Design by inari

Contents

Illustrations

Numerous smaller illustrations

From the 1951 edition:

Affectionately dedicated to Brownies,
Girl Scouts and Girl Guides the World Over

Books in the Young Patriots Series

Watch for more Young Patriots Coming Soon
Visit www.patriapress.com for Updates!

Chapter 1

The Little Rebel

The morning sun peeped through a tall window in one of the big front bedrooms of the William Gordon home in Savannah, Georgia. It touched the eyes of the two little sisters sleeping in a high four-poster bed.

Daisy, who was not quite five, woke at once and sat up. She heard her mother talking in a low voice to the nurse.

"I hope the children sleep late," she was saying. "We'll never leave if I have to answer Daisy's questions."

Daisy slid out of bed and ran into the hall. She left seven-year-old Nellie still asleep.

"What questions will I ask?" she demanded.

"Oh, Daisy, are you up?" said Mrs. Gordon. "What an early bird you are! Come with me so we

1

won't wake Nellie and baby Alice."

She led Daisy to her own room and closed the door. She tucked her into her own bed and sat beside her.

"Now, Daisy Dee, I'm going to tell you something very exciting," she began. "You know that General Sherman and his Yankees captured our city of Savannah last week, don't you?"

"Of course I do," answered Daisy. "I know all about our War between the States. I know that Papa is fighting for the Con-fed-er-a-cy—that's the South. I know that my three uncles, your brothers, Mamma, are fighting for Mr. Lincoln—that's the North. I know our soldiers are called Rebels and wear gray uniforms. The enemies wear blue uniforms. They are mean old Yankees and I hate them."

Daisy stopped to take a breath. Mrs. Gordon was sorry to learn that her middle-sized daughter knew so much about the war. She had tried to keep the war away from her little girls. "You were born just when the cruel war was beginning, dear," she said. "That was in 1860, and now it's 1865. Oh how I pray it may end soon!"

"I know some people say you're a Yankee, Mamma," said Daisy. "That makes me and Nellie awful mad. I tell them you're the rebelest Rebel in the South, even if Grandma and Grandpa Kinzie

She led Daisy to her own room and closed the door.
She tucked her into her own bed and sat beside her.

do live in Chicago. I tell them that when you married Papa that made you want to be a Rebel. That's
so, isn't it, Mamma?"

"Of course, dear. Now let me tell my news," said
Mrs. Gordon. "General Sherman has ordered all
women and children out of Savannah. When he
came to see us the other day . . ."

"Why did you let him, Mamma?" cried Daisy.

"That's why people think we're Yankees. I wish I hadn't eaten that old sugar he gave me and Nellie. But it was good and I never saw sugar before."

"Now, Daisy, let me talk, dear," said Mrs. Gordon. "When General Sherman was here I asked permission to go through his lines to visit our Southern soldiers. I wanted to see Papa. The general said I might and gave me a pass. I saw Papa last night."

"You went right through the Yankee army? You saw Papa and we didn't? That wasn't fair," cried Daisy. "Is he coming home right away? Tell me quick."

"I will, Juliette, if you'll just be quiet," said Mrs. Gordon.

Daisy put her hand over her mouth and nodded. When Mamma called her by her real name she knew she must listen.

"Papa wants you and Nellie and baby Alice and me to go on a long visit to Chicago, to see Grandpa and Grandma Kinzie. We'll go on a boat to New York and then a train from New York to Chicago. We are going today!"

Daisy couldn't speak for a second. She had so many questions she didn't know which to ask first. Just then the door opened and Nellie came in. She was still yawning but she quickly woke up at the news. When the nurse came in a minute later with two-year-old Alice in her arms, Nellie was almost as excited as Daisy.

"Weren't you scared when you went right through the Yankee lines?" she asked. "Weren't you afraid they might shoot you, Mamma?"

"No, dear. I couldn't have gone North without seeing Papa. I wanted to be sure that his wound was healing," Mrs. Gordon answered. "Now, Daisy, once Nurse has you ready to go, you must keep clean. Liza Hendry is washing your other dress now. Mose has gone to tell your Aunt Margaret, and I'm sure the children will all come back here with her. Then you and Nellie can tell them the news."

Mose, Nurse and Liza Hendry were former slaves. Until 1863, when all the slaves were set free under the Emancipation Proclamation, the Gordon family had owned them, and they had to work as their servants. They had also taken care of Captain William Gordon, the children's father, when he was a little boy.

Aunt Margaret Anderson's family arrived almost at once. There were five Anderson children. The youngest, Randy and Sadie, were Nellie's and Daisy's best friends.

The Andersons had already had their meager

breakfast. They waited in the parlor while the Gordons ate theirs. Nellie and Daisy went to eat their little bowls of mush. Madam Gordon, Papa's mother, was already at the table in her high-backed chair.

"You should have milk and sugar to eat with your mush," she said. "But all we have must go to our brave Southern soldiers, if the Yankees don't get it first. You gobbled up the sugar which that Yankee general gave you."

"Are you going to Chicago with us, Grandma?" Daisy suddenly asked.

"No, Juliette," said Grandma. "It would take more than an upstart Northern general like William Tecumseh Sherman to get me away from my home."

"But you think it best for us to go, don't you, Mother Gordon?" said Mamma in a worried voice.

"Whatever your husband thinks best is right, Eleanor," said the old lady. "The children need food. They can get very little here."

Suddenly Daisy began to sniff the air like a puppy. "Smell!" She slipped off her chair. "Come on, Nellie, Liza's cooking something special."

All seven cousins raced down into the kitchen in the cellar.

"You all mind me and come in on your toes,"

whispered Liza Hendry, the cook. "Walk light now. I'm going to show you my cake. Don't any of you dance or cut up. Mind!"

One after the other they tiptoed across the wide kitchen to the big iron stove.

"You get right back of me, Miss Daisy, honey," whispered the old woman. "Now stop breathing, all of you."

She carefully opened the stove door. "There now, isn't that pretty?" she said proudly.

"What did you say it was, Liza Hendry?" whispered Nellie.

"A cake, Miss Nellie," said the cook. "It's got a whole egg in it and a cup of sugar! I unburied the sugar, and Mose, he picked up that egg."

"Is cake good to eat?" asked Daisy.

Liza Hendry threw up her hands over her head. "Just listen to you. Almost five years old and you don't know what a cake is," said Liza Hendry. "No wonder my family looks like plucked chickens. No biscuits, no butter, no cream, no cake, no nothing, because the Yankees came to Georgia."

"Liza Hendry, what does this mean?" said Mrs. Gordon sharply from the doorway. "Are you wasting sugar on a cake when our soldiers need every bit we can find a way to take to them? Where did you get it?"

She carefully opened the stove door. "There now, isn't that pretty?" she said proudly.

Liza Hendry put her hands on her hips and her eyes flashed. "Don't you tell me anything about my kitchen, Miss Eleanor! I buried that sugar away from the Yankees. And I unburied that sugar for a teeny-weeny cake for my going-away family."

Mrs. Gordon had sudden tears in her eyes. She patted Liza Hendry on the shoulder.

The children looked at one another and ran back upstairs. "I know how mad Liza Hendry can get all of a sudden," Nellie said, "but I never heard her speak like that to a grownup."

Mrs. Gordon soon came up the stairs smiling and sent them all running errands for her up and downstairs and in and out of doors.

No one saw Daisy slip out of the house alone, heading for the playhouse.

The neighborhood playhouse was under the spreading branches of a giant pittosporum bush near a live oak tree. There were two little pretend rooms under the bush. Elizabeth, Daisy's doll, and Ophelia, Nellie's doll, were in one of the rooms.

She carried Ophelia carefully because Nellie was always so careful with her. But she gave Elizabeth's cracked face a big kiss and then tucked her carelessly under her arm.

As she started slowly back to the house, she realized that she would not see home again for a long time. From where she stood she could see her own bedroom window above a magnolia tree. Smoke was coming out of the chimneys of the three cabins in which Nurse, Liza Hendry, and Mose lived. Daisy walked to the small iron gate and had a good swing back and forth.

Then she hurried on to the house. She had a lump in her throat and tears in her eyes.

When she came into the hall she heard Randy Anderson talking to Nellie.

"Only Yankees eat like that," he was saying. "But then I guess you all are Yankees now. At least Aunt Eleanor probably is. General Sherman came to see her."

He could say no more. Daisy had butted him in the stomach. He doubled up. Then he sat down hard and tried to defend himself from her fists and feet.

"Take that back!" she shouted. "My mamma is the rebelest Rebel in the whole world and you know it, Jefferson Randolph Anderson! You know Mr. Yankee Sherman came to see her because he is friends with Grandpa Kinzie in Chicago. You know we hate Yankees!"

"My, my, what's going on?" asked Liza Hendry, as she came panting up the stairs. "You know I don't hold with fighting, Miss Daisy. Get yourself right up from there. Now we're goin' to eat the little cake. Miss Nellie, you're the smart one. You count and see how many pieces I'm going to need to cut. It ain't bigger than my hand, that cake ain't. Baby Alice wants a piece too."

Nellie was pleased. She counted everyone—six Andersons, four Gordons, Mose, Nurse and Liza Hendry herself.

Daisy nibbled a little bit off the top of hers and put the rest into her pocket. She always saved a bit of something she really liked for another time.

"There's the livery-stable carriage," called Nellie. "Oh, Mamma, we can't go in that! Look at that awful horse. You can see its ribs."

The Gordons and Andersons had given all the best horses to the Southern army long ago.

"Poor thing, it's just hungry!" said Daisy.

The whole group went down the walk together. Randy stuck close to Daisy's side.

"Don't get to liking Yankees, Daisy," he whispered.

"Of course I won't," answered Daisy. "Not unless I want to."

Mose soon had the few bags in the carriage. He helped the family into their seats—all but Daisy. Daisy was missing.

"She was feeding my horse something," said the

old driver. "Here she comes now."

"I just gave him what was left of my cake," said Daisy, skipping up to the carriage. "He said 'thank you.' He told me that he gets mighty hungry now the Yankees have come to town."

The rickety old carriage started. No one looked back, but Daisy hung out as far as she could, looking forward.

"I'm going to be the first one to see the boat," she called to Mrs. Gordon.

Chapter 2

Up in Yankee Land

The trip north was very hard for everybody. There was hardly a day of the long voyage to New York when anyone could go out on deck because of the storms and the cold January wind.

The train ride from New York to Chicago was long and dirty.

Grandpa and Grandma Kinzie met the little family at the station. Then everyone felt better.

Grandma was short and roundfaced with twinkling blue eyes. Grandpa was tall and thin with dark eyes like Nellie's and Daisy's.

Soon they were all tucked under warm buffalo robes in Mr. Kinzie's carriage. A fine team of brown horses carried them rapidly along the cobblestone streets and dirt roads. Soon they reached his farm—a square, comfortable-looking

A fine team of brown horses carried them rapidly along the cobblestone streets and dirt roads.

house facing Lake Michigan.

"Whoo-woo!" Grandpa shouted. "We're here."

Bridget, the cook, and a big Saint Bernard dog came hurrying down the walk together.

"Oh, you beautiful!" squealed Daisy, running to meet the dog. "I didn't know there was a dog to play with, Grandpa. What's his name?"

"Duke," said Bridget. "And I know your name. It's Daisy."

Daisy had to stand on tiptoe to reach Duke's collar.

"It's amusing to see a little thing like Daisy not afraid of a dog like Duke," said Mr. Kinzie proudly. "Has she seen one like him before?"

"She isn't afraid of anything at all," said Nellie. "She can climb right up on top of the barn at home and not fall off."

"Sort of like her mamma," Grandpa chuckled.

Inside the house was warm and cozy. There was a huge fireplace in the snug sitting room. A big fire roared up the chimney. As soon as their coats were off, Bridget brought in some hot milk and the cookie jar.

Daisy, who had been looking at everything in the room, hurried back to the fireplace. "Me first!" she cried. "Do the cookies have faces, Bridget?"

"Tut-tut," said Grandma. "Grownups first, my child." She smiled over her steel-rimmed glasses at Daisy.

"No, us first," said the little girl. "We're the hungriest."

"I'm afraid they're spoiled, Mother," said Mrs. Gordon. "We've had so little food for so long that children always come first."

"I'd forgotten, dear," Grandma said. "Nellie, you may pass the jar to all of us. You are the oldest."

Daisy was angry. She stood with her hands behind her back and watched Nellie pass the cookie jar. When it came her turn she put both her hands in the jar at once.

"I'll have the most anyway." She giggled. Daisy Gordon could never stay angry for any length of time.

"Don't eat too many," said Bridget. "I'm going right now to put my biscuits in the oven. We're going to have fried chicken, Miss Nell."

"We'll go with you," said Daisy. "Come on, Nellie."

Duke followed them. Baby Alice began to cry. Daisy flew back to her and took her hand.

"Don't you cry, Alice, sister is going to take you too," she said.

When supper was ready, the older girls sat on top of a big book which he had put on their chairs. Allie was almost asleep on her mother's lap. Duke lay on the floor near his new friend.

The biscuits were just in front of Daisy. She reached for two and gave one to Nellie.

"Let's fold our hands first while Grandpa says grace," said Grandma.

"Oh, Mother, I'm afraid we've left so many of the nice things out of their training since the war began. It's good we came here for a while," said Mamma.

Nellie and Daisy folded their hands as the grownups had. But they peeked out while Grandpa spoke to see what everyone was doing.

"It's just like Sunday school," Daisy whispered.

Such a supper! There was fried chicken and biscuits and gravy and milk and jelly and apple pie. Nellie and Daisy could eat very little. But they tasted everything.

"It's better that way, Papa," explained Mrs. Gordon. "Their stomachs are so shrunk from lack of food that they have no room for more now, but they'll soon clean up their plates."

For some time Grandma had been watching Daisy. She saw her slip a biscuit, a chicken leg and then her piece of pie into her lap. She guessed that the food was for Duke.

"Child, why are you doing that?" she finally asked. "Bridget feeds Duke in the kitchen. And he doesn't like pie."

"It's not for Duke. It's for Papa. I'm going to send it to him," Daisy explained. "I don't know how I'll get it to him in the Rebel army, but I'll find a way."

"Oh, if we only could." Her mother sighed.

By the time supper was over the travelers were all yawning.

"I'm going up those stairs I saw in the sitting room and see where our bed is," said Daisy.

"Come on, Nellie! Come on, Duke! You come too, Mamma, and bring Allie."

Before the grandfather clock struck seven the Gordons were all tucked in warm feather beds.

"I just love Grandpa and Grandma and Bridget and Duke," said Daisy sleepily to her sister by her side. "They aren't real Yankees at all."

Chapter 3

"The Ground is Covered with Sugar"

Before she had her eyes open the next morning Mrs. Gordon heard Daisy screaming. She jumped out of bed and met Grandpa and Grandma in the hall.

"What can have happened?" said Mrs. Kinzie. "Maybe the poor child had a bad dream."

Just then Nellie and Daisy rushed out of their room. "Mamma! Mamma! Mamma!" they cried. "The ground is covered with sugar."

"We're going right out and get lots of it to eat," said Nellie. "And, Mamma, we're going to send lots and lots of it home to everybody."

The grownups began to laugh. Mrs. Gordon put her arms about the two shivering little girls and led them downstairs into the warm sitting room. They ran to the window.

"Look, Mamma! You can't see anything but sugar," said Daisy.

"Children, that is snow," explained Mrs. Gordon. "Don't you remember I told you what fun it was to make a snowman at Grandpa's? We had a heavy snowstorm in the night. Isn't it beautiful?"

"Are you sure, Mamma?" said Nellie. "It looks just like the sugar General Sherman gave us."

"There's Duke playing in it. Dress us quick so we can play with him," said Daisy, jumping up and down.

"Honey, it's so cold out there you'd freeze in your light clothes," said Mrs. Gordon. "You'll have to wait until I can buy you some warm ones."

"I don't know about that, Nell," said Grandma, with twinkles in her blue eyes. "Shut your eyes tight, children, and count to a hundred. Don't you peep."

"Maybe Grandma is a fairy with a magic wand," Daisy giggled.

Nellie said nothing. She was counting. It was quite a while before she shouted, "One hundred!"

"Open your eyes," said Grandma Kinzie.

"Grandma! You are a fairy. I know you are," gasped Daisy.

And no wonder. Grandma and Bridget had made warm clothes for all of their guests. Some of them

20

were too large, but that didn't matter. They were the first *new* clothes that Daisy could remember.

When they were dressed they had breakfast. Then on went their new coats and hoods, mittens, and boots. It was too cold for Allie to go out. She stayed at the window with Mamma and watched.

"All right, here we go," said Grandpa, beaming at them. "Now listen to me carefully. There may be drifts out in the yard—that is, deeper snow in some places than in others. You two stay right on the porch until I call you."

Daisy and Nellie could hardly get their breath, it was so cold and windy.

"I'm going out and play with Duke," Daisy said. "I didn't promise to stay here."

She stepped quickly down into the soft snow. It came halfway up her boot legs. She gasped and plodded on.

Suddenly she felt herself going down, down. She yelled. She tried to fight her way out, but she sank up to her shoulders and then to her chin in snow.

Grandpa came running, but Duke got there first. In only a few seconds he had rescued his new friend and was shaking her. He had learned how to deal with snow in faraway Switzerland. When Grandpa carried Daisy into the house, she was still sobbing. "It ate me up. It ate me up!" she cried. "I couldn't get away from it."

Mamma comforted her. Duke stood nearby, wagging his tail and looking worried. Soon Daisy's smile appeared. "Did I fall into a drift, Grandpa?"

"You did," answered Grandpa. "How did you like it?"

"I didn't like it a bit," answered Daisy. "I'll stay on the porch next time."

"Want to go out again?" Grandpa asked.

"Right away," said Daisy, her eyes sparkling. "I'll hold onto Duke's collar this time."

They built a wonderful snowman right outside the sitting-room window where Alice and Mamma and Grandma could watch them. They put a stocking cap on the snowman's head and a scarf about his neck and a pipe in his mouth.

They hung a small basket of crumbs over his arm. "We will keep the basket filled for the birds," Grandpa explained.

As he spoke there was the sound of bells. A big sleigh drawn by a prancing brown horse drew up before the gate.

"That's your aunt, Mrs. John Kinzie, and your cousin, Johnny," said Grandpa. "Come on, we'll go meet them. I expect they've come to visit."

Johnny frowned and shook his head when his mother wanted him to get out. Suddenly Daisy

They built a wonderful snowman right outside the
sitting-room window. . .

stooped down and looked carefully at the runners of the sleigh. "Where are the wheels on your carriage?" she asked.

"Don't you know anything at all, you Rebel?" Johnny said. "Sleighs don't have wheels."

Daisy's eyes flashed. She doubled up her fists. "Are you a Yankee?" she asked. "If you are, I won't let you come in the house."

"I'll come if I like," said the boy. "You can't keep me out."

"I can so," said Daisy.

"You'd better watch out, Johnny," said Nellie. "She can bite and kick pretty hard."

"Now that will do," said Mr. Kinzie sternly. "There'll be no more talk about Yankees and Rebels in my house or yard while the Gordons are here. Is that understood, John? Is that understood, Daisy and Nellie?"

The children looked at one another.

"But those old Rebels killed my father," said Johnny. "I hate Rebels."

"Oh!" said Daisy. "Honest? Won't he ever come back any more?"

Johnny Kinzie shook his head. "He was the bravest soldier in the whole Yankee army and your folks killed him," he said fiercely.

Daisy's eyes grew big. "Your soldiers hurt my

father, but they didn't kill him," she said slowly. "I'm sorry about your father, Johnny. Honest I am." And suddenly she felt very sorry for Grandma and Grandpa who had lost a son in the war. And for her mother who had lost a brother even if he had been a Yankee.

Chapter 4

Little-Ship-Under-Full-Sail

Daisy was sick. One night she was so hot Mamma couldn't keep the covers over her. She moaned in her sleep. Finally Grandpa put on his snowshoes and walked ten miles to get Dr. Wellings. Dr. Wellings lived clear across town.

When they returned Daisy was worse. "She has a brain fever, Nell," the doctor soon said to Mrs. Gordon. "It is very, very serious."

Day after day and week after week went by. Then one evening Nellie heard Bridget say that Daisy was going to die. She was so scared that Grandma drew her onto her lap and comforted her.

Grandpa read the Bible. Then he and Grandma and Bridget prayed on their knees in the kitchen. Nellie thought about the picture of the kind-faced Jesus in the Sunday school room at home. She prayed too. Dr. Wellings and Mamma stayed all night with Daisy.

In the morning Daisy was better.

But the snow was gone before Daisy had another chance to play in it. Even when she was almost well she was still too weak to walk. Grandpa carried her wherever she wanted to go. The grownups all waited on her. Neighbors brought her little presents.

In the evenings Grandpa told the most wonderful stories the children had ever heard. They were about little boys and girls who lived in India, China, Japan, Germany, France and England. Grandpa had a wonderful book, too, which was filled with pictures of these children.

One day Daisy found a picture of a very fierce-looking man with feathers in his long hair. He had a club in his hand. There was a house burning in the background.

"That's an Indian warrior," Grandpa explained. "Some Indians live right out in our woods today, but they don't look much like that picture."

"Do they . . . do they burn houses?" whispered Nellie.

"Not now, Nellie," said Grandpa.

"Why? Why would they do anything so dreadful?" asked Daisy.

"They were angry," Grandpa answered, "because

In the evenings Grandpa told the most wonderful stories the children had ever heard.

the white men had taken their hunting grounds from them.

"Did I ever tell you how some Indians stole your great-grandmother when she was a little girl like you? And how they kept her with them until she was quite grown-up?"

"No, you didn't," cried Daisy. "Tell it *now*."

Mr. Kinzie told them about little Eleanor Lytle and how she was so brave that the Indian chief took her for his sister.

"She learned to do all the things that the Indian children did. She learned bird calls. She learned how to build a campfire, and to make a dress and moccasins of deerskin. She played their games. She almost never walked. She almost always ran," said Grandpa. "She sailed along so fast over the ground that, after she had lived with her Indian brother for several years, he gave her an Indian name which meant Little-Ship-Under-Full-Sail."

"Little-Ship-Under-Full-Sail," said Daisy. "Oh, that's the name I'd like to have when I can run again."

"We used to call your mamma that, Daisy Dee," Grandpa said with a smile. "She was always going full speed ahead, too. You work hard, and learn to walk and run again and I'll call you Little-Ship-under-Full-Sail."

"Is that a true story?" asked Daisy. "Oh, I wish Indians would steal me! I'd like to live in the woods and do the things Little-Ship-under-Full-Sail did."

"Wouldn't you be afraid at night?" asked Nellie. "There are bears and wolves and all sorts of wild things in these woods. Grandpa said so."

"Campfires keep animals away," said Daisy.

Spring came and Daisy could go outside again. The children saw a little calf and a baby colt when they were only a few hours old. They helped Grandpa with the baby chickens. They found the first wild flowers in the woods. Daisy spent hours playing happily there, and Grandpa began to call her Little-Ship-under-Full-Sail as he had promised.

One April evening, the Kinzies and the Gordons were at the supper table when a distant farm bell began to ring. A minute later another bell and then another joined in.

Grandpa, Grandma and Mamma jumped to their feet. Nearby bells were ringing now. Someone down the road began to shout, "The war's over! The war's over! Ring your bell, John Kinzie! The war's over!"

"We won," shouted Daisy and Nellie together. "Now Papa can come home."

"Let's tell Bridget," Daisy cried.

The two little girls raced to the kitchen. Bridget was already outside getting ready to pull the rope of their own bell.

"Let us do it," shouted Daisy. "We won."

The three of them pulled and pulled on the rope and Grandpa's bell rang out with the others. Now the neighbors began to stream into the yard. The women were hugging one another and crying. The men tossed their hats into the air.

"We've licked those Rebels. Hurrah for General Grant!" someone shouted.

"God bless the Union! Hurrah for Abraham Lincoln and General Grant!" someone shouted.

"We've won the war!"

Mrs. Gordon hurried to the little girls and put an arm about each of them.

"Why do they say those things?" asked Daisy, her eyes flashing. "Tell them we won the war, Mamma. Papa said we would."

"No, dear," answered Mrs. Gordon quietly. "The Yankees won. Our brave men fought as long and as hard as they could, but they did not win."

"But Papa said . . . we . . . would," Nellie sobbed.

"This time Papa was mistaken," said Mamma. "Now don't let anyone see us cry, children. We must be brave. Papa would want us to be."

"The Battle-Hymn of the Republic," someone shouted, "sing it out. Sing it!"

The crowd gathered about the leader.

"Mine eyes have seen the glory of the
coming of the Lord;
He is trampling out the vintage where

the grapes of wrath are stored;
He hath loosed the fateful lightning of
his terrible swift sword;
His truth is marching on.
 Glory Glory Hallelujah!
 Glory Glory Hallelujah!
 Glory Glory Hallelujah!
 His truth is marching on."

The crowd sang all the stanzas. When they stopped for breath a high little voice, singing all alone, began another song.

"I wish I was in Dixie! Hooray! Hooray!
In Dixie land we'll take our stand, to live and die in Dixie,
Away, away, away down south in Dixie!"

For a minute no one moved. Daisy stood up on the fence holding to the post. Grandpa went over and lifted her to his shoulder. She sang her song straight through.

"Hurrah for the little Rebel!" a neighbor shouted. "She's got spunk."

"Hurrah for our great Southern general, Robert E. Lee!" Daisy shouted back. "Hurrah for all our gray soldiers! Hurrah for my papa!"

Grandpa went over and lifted her to his shoulder. She sang her song straight through.

Chapter 5

Home Again

It was midsummer before Captain Gordon could come for his family. He looked very thin and sad. He still wore his gray uniform because he had no other suit.

Papa was in a great hurry to get back to Savannah. "We have a long struggle ahead of us," he told Grandpa Kinzie. "The soldiers have left our fields bare, our stables empty, and our homes need repairs. We must hurry back and get started all over again."

Soon they were ready to leave. Daisy's pockets were full of shells and stones. She carried a box of cookies and a box of scraps for doll clothes. She had a tiny maple tree under her arm. Tucked into the tops of her shoes were two feathers.

There was a present for everyone she loved at home.

"You look like Santa Claus," Grandma said.

"Little Ship, you won't forget the promise you made Grandpa, will you?" said Mr. Kinzie seriously.

"About not hating the Yankees and liking all kinds of people?" said Daisy. "Of course I won't. I promised."

"And keep your sails flying, won't you," Grandpa whispered. "Now, goodbye, all of you. Come again soon. We won't know what to do without our little Southerners."

The journey home was pleasant. When they reached their house in Savannah the Andersons were all there to greet them.

"Randy," Daisy said at once. "I don't hate Yankees any more. Do you?"

"Of course I do," he answered with a scowl. "You'd better change your mind if you want to play with me."

"I can't," said Daisy. "I told Grandpa Kinzie I'd be friends with Yankees and Rebels and Indians and everybody else. I promised."

"All right, I don't care," shouted Randy. "I don't want to play with girls any more anyhow."

He raced off down the street.

"Well, he'll be sorry when he knows I brought him some shells for his collection," said Daisy. "I brought you some scraps for doll clothes, Sadie, and some cookies for everyone. Where's Mose?"

"He and Liza Hendry and Nurse are waiting in the hall," said Aunt Margaret. "Grandma Gordon is in the parlor waiting too."

"Oh, my goodness!" said Daisy in a worried voice. "I forgot to bring her a present. What shall I do?"

"Come along now, honey," said Papa. "Grandma won't mind."

"I brought you a little maple tree, Mose," Daisy said. "Do you know what? Grandpa says its leaves turn red in the fall. This is a bluejay's feather, Liza Hendry, and here's one from a cardinal's tail, Nurse. They're for luck, you know."

"Come along now, children," said Mamma. "Do you remember how to curtsy?"

"I do, and I taught Allie too," said Nellie proudly. "Come on, baby, show Grandma how nice you can bob."

Daisy was digging into her pockets. Suddenly she found what she was hunting for. She followed the others into the drawing room.

Grandma Gordon sat in her high-backed chair. She wore a black satin dress, a white lace cap, and earrings. She was delighted to see the grownups. She smiled when little Allie bobbed before her. She nodded in approval over Nellie's curtsy.

"And Juliette, how are you?" she said to Daisy. Daisy had suddenly noticed the piano. Its two front legs were off and it was balanced on boxes.

"Grandma Gordon, did those mean old Yankees break Mamma's piano? Did they? I hate—"

"Daisy, you promised Grandpa," Nellie reminded her.

Daisy's eyes flashed for a minute. She started to answer back and then gulped. She pushed a gray stone with a red mark around it into Madam Gordon's hand. "It's for you," she said, and ran out of the room.

Sadie Anderson was waiting in the hall and the two hurried off together.

"Let's go see the playhouse," said Daisy. "Did you take good care of it?"

"Yes, but your grandma was the one who saved it from being cut down," said Sadie.

"Grandma?" Daisy cried. "Why, how could she? What happened?"

By this time the two little girls were running down the path to the great pittosporum bush. They ducked under the branches and Daisy smiled with happiness. "It's just the same as ever," she said. "Tell me what Grandma did."

"Well, Randy and I saw three Yankee soldiers go in through the iron gate one day. They had an ax and a saw. They cut down the live oak by the hedge and then they went over to this one," began Sadie. She pointed to the big tree by the playhouse.

"Let's take this oak and the bush too," one of them said. "Its branches will make a good kindling."

"Then we saw Grandma Gordon coming down the path from the house," Sadie went on. "You know how straight she walks? Well, she stopped right in front of the men.

"'Gentlemen,' she said, 'you'll take no more from this yard. Is it your custom to make war on children as well as women? That bush is my grandchildren's playhouse.'

"'Can't help it, lady,' said one soldier. 'It's ours now. Go ahead, Jim. Cut them both down, the tree and the bush.'

"Then Grandma Gordon took her cane and pretty near broke it whacking that Yankee's shoulder. He yelled and the three of them skedaddled."

Daisy's eyes sparkled. She looked up at the house. Mrs. Gordon was standing by the parlor window with Grandma.

Daisy jumped up and down. She waved and pointed to the playhouse and waved again. "Grandma smiled. I saw her," she said.

The first week or so Daisy spent calling on the

neighbors. She told them all about her illness, and about Grandpa and Grandma Kinzie. She had a wonderful time.

"Now if Randy would just play with us everything would be scrumptious," she said happily.

Chapter 6

First Day at School

It was October when Daisy and Sadie started off together for their first day in school.

"Are you scared?" Sadie asked as they hurried down the street. "I don't think I can learn to read."

"I can read now," said Daisy proudly. "But I can't spell or do sums."

"Hello, Yankee," shouted Randy as he ran by them. "Bet you're scared of Miss Blois. You ought to be. Just wait until she gets mad at you!"

Daisy and Sadie looked at each other. Daisy giggled "Pooh, that's not what Nellie told me," she said.

Miss Lucile Blois was the teacher. She had a small private school in her own home. Most of the children Daisy knew went there. Some of their parents had gone to Miss Blois too.

She was a little old lady. She wore a plum-colored silk dress. A very large gold pin fastened her lace collar.

When the two little girls reached the school Miss Blois was standing at the door to greet her old and new pupils.

"She doesn't look fierce," Sadie whispered.

"It's not hard to guess your last name, my child," the teacher said with a smile. "No one could mistake you for a younger sister of Elise and Meta Anderson. You're Sarah, aren't you?"

Sadie nodded. She couldn't speak.

"And you're a Gordon," Miss Blois said to Daisy. "Let me see—I don't think I know your name. Would you tell me what it is?"

"My real name, or my play name, or my Indian name?" Daisy answered pertly.

"Oh, I know. It's Juliette. A little bird told me that Juliette Gordon had bad manners. But I don't believe it," Miss Blois said with a nice smile. "You look too much like your lovely mother, my dear, not to be a real lady."

Daisy was so surprised that for once she could think of nothing to say.

The pupils sat in the big room according to their age. The youngest were nearest the teacher. Daisy and Sadie had a double desk together in the front row. Miss Blois waited until everyone had had a chance to greet everyone else. Then she sat down at the piano. At the first notes of "Dixie" the children jumped to their feet and stood very straight.

Daisy's high little voice carried on through stanza after stanza.

"You know all the words, don't you, my child?" said the teacher. "That is fine."

"I sang it all through by myself up in Chicago on the day the war was over," said Daisy proudly. "There were a lot of Yankees in my Grandpa Kinzie's yard and they sang their war song first. Then I sang 'Dixie,' and I said 'Hurrah for Robert E. Lee and for our gray soldiers and for Papa!'"

Miss Blois smiled. She leaned over and patted Daisy's head. "I thought the little bird who told me you're a Yankee was wrong," she said.

"You know a great many birds, don't you?" said Daisy.

Everybody in the room laughed and even Miss Blois smiled.

"Daisy Gordon, what would Mamma say?" said Nellie.

"I don't think Juliette meant to be rude, Eleanor," said Miss Blois. "Did you, my child?"

Daisy giggled and shook her head.

"Randy, please pass out the copybooks," said Miss

Blois. "Pupils, get out your spellers and pencils."

Daisy watched Randy hurry to the closet for the books. Then he started down the aisle by her desk. "Now you'll be in trouble, Miss Yankee," he whispered as he went by.

Daisy said nothing, but when he came back to get more copybooks he suddenly fell down. He got up at once and glared at Daisy. She glared back.

"Juliette, do you know why Randy fell down?" asked Miss Blois.

"I tripped him," Daisy answered. "He called me a Yankee. I won't let anyone do that. I like my Yankee friends, but I'm not a Yankee."

Miss Blois looked from one angry child to the other. Then she sat down on the chair behind her desk.

"The school may put down their pencils and sit up straight," she said quietly. "I will not begin the school year with hard feelings between pupils. Juliette, you may tell us about your Yankee friends. Then I'm sure we'll understand why you like them."

Daisy was so surprised that for a minute she couldn't speak, but she soon found her tongue. "I love my Grandpa and Grandma Kinzie because they are kind and lots of fun," she began. "They hated the war but they didn't hate us even though

"Juliette, do you know why Randy fell down?"

Uncle John was killed fighting us. He's their son."

"Why did the Yanks start the war?" asked an older boy.

"I don't know anything about that," said Daisy in a puzzled voice. "But Grandpa says that the Northern soldiers fought because they believed in what they were fighting for. And he said our men fought for the very same reason. That's queer, isn't it?

"Then there was Bridget, Grandma's cook; Dr. Wellings who took care of me when I was so sick; and all the neighbors who brought me presents. They are all friends of mine. I like them all because I know them. Grandpa says that's what counts."

"Then you do like all of them better than us, don't you?" said Randy.

"Of course I don't," cried Daisy. "You know I don't, Jefferson Randolph Anderson. I love our Rebels best of all, but I'm always going to have friends in different places. Maybe even across the ocean when I'm grown up."

"I think she's telling the truth, Randy," said his friend, David Morton. "If she is, then you ought to beg her pardon. You told all of us she liked Yankees best, and that she was a Yankee herself."

"Well, I thought so," said Randy. "General Sherman did go to see her folks. He didn't go to see anyone else."

"You know why," said David and Daisy together.

"I guess so," said Randy.

"Well," said David, "are you a Southern gentleman or not?"

"Of course he is," said Daisy, jumping to her feet. "Don't you dare say he isn't, David Morton."

Her eyes flashed and she pushed her way to Randy's side. She was ready to defend him against anyone else. Randy's face flushed and he put out his hand. "I'm sorry, Daisy," he said.

"Oh, that's all right," said Daisy. She glared at David before she took her seat.

But at recess she was as happy as any little girl could be—a girl who loved everybody and wanted to play in every game.

The rest of the day in school was not nearly so much fun as the first part. Daisy had to learn how to spell ten words. She missed nine of them because she was watching two birds outside the window.

She started on her table of 3's. But just when she began to whisper "two times three is six," the seventh graders took out their pencils and paper and began to draw.

Daisy took hers from her desk and began to draw too. She made a picture of the birds. She forgot all about the 3's.

Miss Blois was watching her. Before school was dismissed the teacher put the names up on the board of all those who had a hundred on their papers. Sadie's name and Nellie's name were there. Daisy's wasn't.

Daisy wrinkled her forehead and looked unhappy for a minute. Then she showed Miss Blois her picture of the two birds.

"Can't I have a hundred for this?" she asked.

"That's very nice, Daisy, but the first grade didn't have drawing today," said Miss Blois. "In school we do as we're told. That's a very important part of it, my child."

"Oh," said Daisy. "Like the army. We have to take orders. Are you the general, Miss Blois?"

Daisy was serious, but the other pupils all laughed. So did the teacher. It was funny to think of little Miss Blois as a general.

"No, child, I'm just the captain," said Miss Blois. "Good night, Private Gordon."

"Good night, sir." Daisy giggled. "I'll be back tomorrow."

Chapter 7

The Lady from Japan

Most of Miss Blois' pupils went to Sunday school at Old Christ Church on Johnson Square. Daisy liked going there almost more than day school. Miss Anne, her teacher, had once been a missionary.

Miss Anne was like Grandpa Kinzie. She said that all the people in the world could be friends if they only knew one another well enough. She said that most little girls she had known liked the same things, whether their skins were white or dark or yellow. She still received letters from Japan and Korea and India, where she had lived.

When Daisy listened to Miss Anne tell a story she forgot she was sitting with Sadie and her other friends. She felt she was right there in the foreign land.

One rainy Sunday when the three Gordons reached the church, they saw Miss Anne talking to a strange woman. The stranger had black hair, with long gold pins in it. She wore a gray dress with loose, full sleeves.

"It looks like Mamma's wrapper," Daisy whispered. "What funny eyes she has, all slanty! But pretty."

The bell rang and Miss Anne introduced the guest. "Children, when I was in Japan, I lived next door to Miss Osawa," she said. "She and I have been good friends for many years. After we sing our songs for her, she is going to tell us about the Japanese children."

Daisy left her seat in the fourth row and took an empty one in the front row, even if this did put her with the babies.

Miss Osawa talked about her pupils in her faraway land, and Daisy listened to every word. Then she told about the doll and the silver fish.

"When a little girl is born in my country," Miss Osawa began, "her papa fastens a brightly colored paper doll on a long stick outside the front door. When the neighbors see this they nod their head and say, 'Ah, our new friend is a girl. She will always be played with and cared for like the doll which hangs before the house.'

The stranger had black hair, with long gold pins in it.

"But if a boy baby comes to the house, the father hurries outside with a fish made of silver paper. He puts it on the stick.

"'Yes,'" say the neighbors, 'the little lad will be like a fish. He will always have trouble getting what he wants. He will often swim against the tide as only a man can, but he will win out in the end.'"

"Couldn't girls do that too?" Daisy Gordon asked.

"No, my dear," said Miss Osawa. "There are many things little girls can't do that boys can."

Daisy listened to the rest of the stories with one ear. She was thinking. "That lady can't tell me one thing I can't do that boys can," she whispered to herself.

She was still thinking about this when she, Alice, Nellie, and Sylvia Morton tried to walk under one umbrella.

Sylvia began to argue as soon as Daisy brought up the subject. "What do I care whether it's true or not," Sylvia said. "I don't want to do what boys do, anyhow."

"Neither do I," said Nellie.

"But I do," said Daisy. "And I will."

"Don't be silly, Daisy," said Sylvia. "I don't want to swim against the tide, even in a story."

Daisy and Nellie looked at each other and giggled. They knew how timid Sylvia was. She always screamed when she went swimming and got beyond her depth.

It had been raining for several days, and the gutters were like streams. At one particularly bad place, the sidewalk was high above the street and the water flowed swiftly toward a drain. "We'd better take off our shoes and stockings and wade like the boys," Daisy said. "We will not," said Sylvia. "You do say the silliest things."

"Hold my hand, Allie. You might slip and fall. We'll have to turn back and go around the block," said Nellie.

"Randy and David are wading," said Daisy. "I'm going to."

She quickly took off her shoes and stockings, pulled her dress up about her knees and waded in. The other girls had already gone back. "You can't go wading, Daisy Gordon," shouted Randy. "You go with the other girls. It's not ladylike."

Daisy paid no attention. The water was cold. A high wind made tiny waves in it. Suddenly she saw a tiny animal bobbing along ahead of her.

She started after it. She shouted, "Randy, Randy, grab it! It's coming past you. It's a kitten or a mouse or something. It's alive!"

The boys were sailing stick boats. They paid no attention to her. Daisy floundered and fell into the water, but she was up again in a minute. She dropped her shoes and stockings in the mud.

Daisy stopped shouting. "Don't worry, kitty," she said with tight lips. "I'll get you myself."

The animal swirled quite near her. She saw a little red mouth and tongue and heard a faint mew. "It's a kitten, Randy! Randy! David!" she yelled.

The boys kept on sailing their boats. Daisy scrambled on. Suddenly she saw the kitten was getting nearer and nearer to the drain.

Daisy stopped shouting. "Don't worry, kitty," she said with tight lips. "I'll get you myself."

She pulled up her long dress and tried to run.

When the kitten was swirling around and around, just before the water would drag it down into the drain, Daisy pounced.

She caught the kitten, but she slipped and fell down. She held onto the kitten, but when she tried to get up she fell again in the slippery mud. She threw out her arms and crawled to one side. She lay in the wet mud a few seconds, getting her breath. Then, at last, the boys saw her. They had her up on her feet in no time.

"It's dead," Daisy sobbed, holding out the kitten. "I did so want to save it. It's dead."

"Maybe not. Let me have it," said David. "A cat has nine lives."

David was going to be a doctor like his father. He knew some things the other boys didn't. He carried the kitten to the pavement and laid it across his knee with its head down. Then he began to push on its sides regularly.

Randy and Daisy watched. Water began to trickle from the kitten's mouth. In a little while the animal began to move. Then it opened its eyes.

"There you are, ma'am," David said proudly. "Better get your child into a warm place and feed it."

Daisy smiled and took the dripping baby into her wet arms.

"What happened?" David asked.

Daisy told him.

The boys went home with her to tell the story. "Maybe you won't get punished if we tell your father what you did," said Randy. "You look like a drowned kitten yourself!"

"A boy couldn't have done better," said David.

The three were just inside the front door when Nellie came racing down the stairs. "Daisy! Randy! David!" she called. "We have a new baby brother named Willy. He has red hair. Mamma says you can come right up and see him."

"Just Miss Daisy," called Nurse. "Nobody except her."

Daisy forgot how wet and shivery she felt. She flew up the stairs and into the nursery. Alice was leaning over the side of the old cradle. "He has a red face," she said. "And he cries."

Daisy peeked over her shoulder.

"Can I see Mamma?" Daisy asked. "Where's Papa?"

"In a little while, said Nurse. "Your papa took the doctor home. Where you been, Daisy Gordon? You look a sight. What's that you got—a kitten?"

"Yes, we were both almost drowned," said Daisy. "I'd better get on some dry clothes. I'm ch-chattery."

Nurse soon had both the kitten and Daisy warm

and dry. Then Daisy hurried back to the baby.

"Now we have a little baby and a little kitten too," said Alice. "I want to hold the kitty. Can it be mine, Daisy?"

Daisy was hanging over Willy's cradle. She was glad to have Alice cuddle the kitten. She touched the baby's tiny hands and soft hair. "I'll take care of you lots," she whispered to him. "I'm so glad you're a brother instead of a sister. I'm going right over and tell Sadie you've come." But she stopped at the top of the stairs and wrinkled her forehead, thinking.

"I'll do it," she whispered. "My goodness, I'm glad I went to Sunday school and that Miss Osawa was there!"

She flew back to her room and pulled out her whatnot box from under the bed. She dumped everything out and found a good-sized piece of gray paper. It wasn't silver but it would do.

Carefully she drew the outline of a fish on it and cut it out. Then she hunted up a piece of string and ran downstairs and out of doors. She tied the fish to the front gate and watched it for a minute. The wind did make it look as if it were swimming.

"Now everybody will know we have a *boy* baby," said Daisy.

Just then Sadie and Aunt Margaret came hurrying down the street.

"Sadie, Sadie," shouted Daisy, "we have a boy baby! I fixed his fish. See—it's swimming against the tide."

Chapter 8

The TAC's

"My goodness, Sadie," said Daisy on the first day of summer vacation. "I just don't have time to take care of all of my animals! I wish Nellie wouldn't bother taking music and dancing lessons, so she could help more." Mr. Gordon had given Daisy an empty stall in the stable in which she could keep her pets. There were two cats, several toads, two frogs, a lame crow, a garter snake, a cocoon in a box and two squirrels that lived in the trees but ate with the others. An owl hooted from the rafters.

"I help a lot," said Sadie. "So does Randy when he can. You don't do it all."

"Sadie, I have an idea," said Daisy suddenly. "Let's have a club and then all the members can help. We could elect a president and have a name just as Mamma's club does. Where's Randy?"

"He's over at David's," said Sadie.

"I don't suppose Sylvia or Nellie will play," said Daisy. "They think they're too grownup."

When Sadie came back she had seven others. The older Anderson children, Meta, Elise, and George, wanted to see what was going on. Nellie and Sylvia came after all, with Randy and David.

Daisy explained her idea, but didn't mention the purpose of the club.

"First we'll elect a president," she said. "I have some paper and a pencil. Each of you write down the name of the person you want to be it. The one who gets the most votes is elected."

"I'll count them," Randy said after everyone had written down a name. "Each paper had a different name," he announced.

Daisy giggled. "I guess everyone voted for himself."

"Never mind, I'll be president," said Randy. "Then we won't have to vote again. We ought to have signals and a secret language."

"I'll be the lady president," said Daisy. "I thought up the club idea. Now we'd better find a name."

"What are we going to do in this club?" asked David.

Sadie and Daisy looked at each other. "Let's find a name first," Daisy said in a loud voice.

"We ought to decide what we're going to do in

the club and then make up the name," insisted David.

"Well, I—thought we—we could *all* take care of my animals, instead of just me," Daisy stammered. Her voice grew surer. "We can catch lots more too. And you can take care of the sick ones, David."

"Then we could call the club 'The Animal Catchers,'" suggested Randy.

"The T.A.C's," said Daisy. "That could be our first secret, because nobody but club members would know what the letters stand for."

"Now we'd better decide on a secret language," said Randy, "like talking backward or putting a special letter before every word."

"Or you can put the letter after the word, like 'I-a want-a to-a have-a club-a.' Say it fast."

They all tried this and then rolled on the ground, because they were laughing so hard.

"We-a better-a have-a signals-a," said Randy. "I-a mean-a like-a blue-a flag-a on-a stick-a says-a 'Come-a over-a at-a once-a,' or-a a red-a one-a for-a cookies-a."

"You-a and-a Meta-a and-a Sylvia-a and Elise-a can-a sew-a them-a for-a us-a," said David.

"I said it would work," whispered Daisy to Sadie. "Now we'd better get them to help clean out the stall."

No one seemed to mind. Soon the animal boxes were out in the sun. The club members were busy making plans for many more pets.

"We ought to have some rules," Daisy said.

"Like what?" asked David.

"Like standing up for one another," said Daisy.

"And being kind to animals," said Sadie.

"And obeying my orders," said Daisy.

"No, mine," said Randy. "I'm the man president."

"Ladies first," Nellie said. "That's being courteous. Courtesy's important."

"When we say we'll do something, we have to do it," said David. "Keeping your word is very important, too."

"That's enough! That's enough!" cried Daisy with her hands over her ears. "We can't be good all the time. Elise had better write the rules down. Then each of us can keep a copy and look at it sometimes."

The first excitement happened to the club the week after it was formed. David and Daisy brought home a stray dog. The club members bathed it, fed it, fixed a box for it and left it for the night.

The next morning when they hurried out to do the chores there were six puppies and a happy mother.

"We can give the pups away as presents," Nellie suggested.

"We can give the pups away as presents," Nellie suggested.

"We can sell them," said Randy.

"We'd better each take one," said Daisy. "Then we'll know it will have a good home."

Kittle, the kitten, caused the next excitement. Shep, the mother dog, chased her up into the live-oak tree. The boys of the club had gone fishing that day with Uncle Bert.

"Just you let that cat be," Mose told Daisy.

"She's going to come down when she gets hungry. Put Sheppie in the barn."

Kittle was at the top of the high tree. Daisy was the only one who seemed worried about her. "I know Randy said I was never to climb his tree," she told herself under her breath, "but this is different. Kittle *needs* me."

Daisy put a box under the lowest branch and pulled herself up. She didn't look down as she climbed. She knew better.

"I'm coming, Kittle," she called softly.

When Daisy had her almost within reach, Kittle began to back away. Daisy coaxed and coaxed, but Kittle just climbed higher, until she was up among the very small branches.

Daisy settled back against the tree trunk. She could see far over the wall into the Andersons' yard and the Mortons' and 'way down Bull Street. Off in the other direction she was sure she could see the river.

"This is a much better 'think' place than the playhouse or the top of the stairs," she said to Kittle. "Thank you lots for showing it to me, even if Randy will be mad."

The boys came home about teatime. They left their fishing poles at their houses and came racing over to the Gordons' yard.

Daisy whistled. They stopped in their tracks. She leaned back against the trunk of the tree and whistled again.

Randy and David whistled back, but they didn't see her at first. Then Kittle began to mew.

"Hey, the cat's up in my tree!" Randy shouted.

"So am I," called Daisy.

Then Randy was angry. He climbed swiftly up after Kittle and glared at Daisy. "Get down out of my tree!" he yelled.

"It's in my yard," Daisy shouted back. "I like it up here."

"Hey, stop fighting. Here come the others," called David. "Now we can tell Daisy, Sadie, and Allie the secret."

The two children forgot their quarrel. They scrambled to the ground. Kittle scampered toward the kitchen and her supper.

Randy called the meeting to order. "We have news for you three little girls," he began. "Aunt Eliza Stiles has asked the rest of us to spend the summer at Etowah Cliffs. You three will be in charge of the animals while we're gone."

"We'd rather go to the farm, wouldn't we, Sadie?" Daisy declared at once.

"Mamma says you are too young this summer," Nellie said. "You'll have to wait and go sometime when she can go too."

"Never mind, Sadie, the animals will like us the best," said Daisy. "I can have the Think Tree to myself too."

The summer was really fun for the stay-at-homes. They played in the playhouse, went on picnics, had their own gardens, and listened to Mamma's stories.

Daisy's favorite story was *The Golden Slippers.* It was a fairy tale about a girl who was shy and thought that no one liked her. Her good fairy felt very sorry for her and gave her a pair of magic golden slippers.

"Wear them whenever you are frightened or shy," said the fairy. "When you have them on your feet remember to be kind to others. Then the slippers will bring you fun, luck, and happiness."

Daisy couldn't remember ever being shy. But she liked the idea of being kind, and she thought it would be nice to have a pair of gold slippers.

Daisy made up rhymes and stories, too, then drew pictures for them. Mamma showed her how to tie the pages together into a book. When Nellie came home she looked through the book. She told Daisy about the magazine their Cousin Caroline and her friends made every summer at Etowah Cliffs. "It's called the *Malbone Bouquet,*" she said.

"That's what I'll do when I go up there," Daisy said at once. "I'll write pieces for it. Would she let me, Nellie?"

"I guess so, but it's hard work and you have to write a lot," said Nellie. "I wouldn't like it."

"I know I would," said Daisy.

Chapter 9

I Say I Won't

Grandma Gordon had asked Daisy and Nellie to have tea in her room.

Daisy fussed and fumed all day. "It's silly," she told Nellie. "Grandma is just trying to teach me manners, and I won't learn."

She and Nellie played together very little nowadays. Daisy was nine and her sister eleven. They liked to do different things.

Nellie was learning to sew. She practiced on the piano and she loved to go to dancing school. Daisy said she'd rather hide for a day than do things like that.

At four o'clock Daisy climbed slowly upstairs to get dressed.

Soon she was knocking on Madam Gordon's door. Nellie opened it. "You're late," she whispered. "Better make a nice curtsy."

Daisy frowned, but she made almost as nice a curtsy as Nellie had. She had decided that she might as well learn, so Grandma would stop pestering her.

Nellie went to sit by Madam Gordon. They picked up their talk where they had left off. Daisy listened a minute. She wasn't interested in what they were saying, and so she got up to look around the room. She found herself face to face with a painting on the wall. It was a portrait of a smiling young girl on a very spirited horse.

"My goodness, that looks like Grandma, almost!" Daisy thought. "It couldn't be, though, because she'd never have ridden such a wild horse."

She went closer and frowned. Then she nodded. "It is Grandma," she said to herself. "I know it is." If she ever smiled it would be like her right now. My goodness, she was brave to ride a horse like that! She doesn't look a bit scared."

"Well, Juliette, when you are through looking over my room, perhaps you'll come and have a cup of tea with Eleanor and me."

"I'll—I'll just have a cookie, thank you, Grandma," Daisy stammered.

"You'll have a cup of tea," said Madam Gordon. "Hold it carefully and take a cookie with your other hand."

Daisy was quite sure she couldn't do that.

"I'll—I'll just have a cookie, thank you, Grandma," Daisy stammered.

Grandma made her nervous, she was so particular. The cup always slipped. It did this time! Tea and cookies tumbled onto the floor.

"You're like a bull in a china shop, Juliette," said Grandma with a frown.

Daisy giggled. This idea had brought a funny picture to her mind. "I know, Grandma," she answered. "I'm sorry, honest I am. I just can't be a lady."

"You are one, Juliette," said Madam Gordon. "You can't help that, but at times you don't act like one."

For the second cup Daisy sat down on a low stool. She felt better. She could have eaten all the cookies on the plate but Grandma passed them only twice and Daisy knew the rules. One cookie each time.

When Daisy had finished Grandma took two small packages from her black satin bag. "I have a present for each of you," she said. "They are earrings which belonged to me when I was a girl. You must take very good care of them."

"I don't want them and I won't wear them," Daisy said promptly.

Grandma frowned but said nothing. She led Nellie over to her washstand. On it were a towel, a cork, a spool of thread, a needle and a little pan. "I will pierce your ears myself so that the holes will be properly placed," said the old lady.

Nellie's face turned white. Daisy's was red.

"Kneel down on this stool, Eleanor," said Grandma firmly. "Turn your head to the side so that I may put the cork under the lobe of your ear. That's right."

Daisy watched Nellie shut her eyes. She saw Grandma raise the needle. But that was all she saw. She ran from the room, down the stairs and out of doors. As she raced by the window on her way to the stable she heard Nellie cry out.

It was dark when Daisy came back to the house. She was dirty, unhappy, and hungry.

She hurried up the back stairs to change for supper. Then she heard Papa laughing in the dining room. The family was already eating supper. No one had missed her. Tears came to Daisy's eyes.

She stepped out of her clothes and left them on the floor. Then she washed her face and climbed into bed.

Nellie came up at nine. She had little white threads hanging from her ears. "I have to pull these threads whenever I think about it," she explained. "If I don't the holes will close up again. It didn't hurt so much. You were a baby."

"You didn't think I was afraid, did you?" said

Daisy. "Well, I wasn't. I just won't wear earrings. It's silly."

Nellie undressed very slowly. She put her clothes neatly away. Then she blew out the candle and got into bed.

"You're funny, Daisy," she said thoughtfully. "Don't you ever want to be a young lady and go to parties and have dresses from New York? Don't you ever think about getting married and . . . things like that?"

"Of course I do," said Daisy. "I'm going to marry a prince. He'll have golden hair and we're going to live in a palace. I'm going to have dozens and dozens of children and a whole stableful of horses."

"I'm going to marry a rich man and have the biggest plantation in the whole South," Nellie confided.

"And you're really not going to sew *all* the time?"

"Goodness no!" said Nellie. "I just want to be able to tell my maid how to sew things right. Besides, sewing is ladylike."

"I'm hungry," Daisy declared. "I'm going down to the pantry and see what's there."

"Bring me a dish of that pudding we had for supper," Nellie whispered. "It was good."

Chapter 10

Daisy's Talisman

"**I** don't care if Grandma doesn't want me in her room, I'm going," Daisy said to herself. "I'm going right now. I'll never draw the horse's front legs right until I see that picture again."

She picked up her sketch, hurried down the hall, and stood breathless before Madam Gordon's closed door. She was scared but determined. She tapped on the door. There was no answer. She knocked on it, and then she banged. Still there was no answer. Then she heard Grandma's cane tapping on the floor and the door opened.

"Is there a fire, Juliette?" said Madam Gordon in a stern voice.

"No, Grandma," answered Daisy. "I just have to look at that picture of you on horseback."

"What picture?" asked Grandma.

"The one I saw on the earring day. I think you were awfully brave to ride such a wild horse. I want to copy how its front legs look when it rears."

Madam Gordon was surprised by this compliment. She closed the door behind her granddaughter. She went back to her chair. Daisy waited a minute for her to speak, but Grandma said nothing. Daisy tiptoed over to the picture.

She sat down on the floor and began to erase her lines. Soon she was so busy that she forgot where she was.

"Juliette, come sit here by me," said Madam Gordon. "I want to talk to you."

Daisy was amazed at her grandmother's kind voice. She went at once. The old lady sat in her high-backed chair as stiff as usual, but she was *smiling*!

"We haven't been very good friends, have we, Juliette?" Madam Gordon began. "Have you ever wondered why?"

"I guess you don't like me much," answered Daisy. "That makes you cross."

"On the contrary, I do like you," said Grandma Gordon. "But you aren't always very pleasant your-self, are you?"

Daisy shook her head.

"I think I probably understand you better than

anyone else in the house, Juliette," Grandma went on. "You are very like me when I was a little girl."

"Like you?"

"Yes," Grandma said with a smile. "What would you think if I told you that when I was your age I wanted to be a jockey on a race track more than anything else in the world?"

"I'd say it was a made-up story," Daisy giggled.

"And I say it's a true story. When I was eleven years old I had my own horse. She was named Glory and I rode her everywhere," said the old lady proudly.

"Honest, Grandma?"

"She was given to me by my grandfather for Christmas."

"I'm almost eleven right now," Daisy said. "Oh, Grandma, do you think Papa can ever, ever afford to give me a horse? If he does, I'm going to call him Fire. He's going to be black as night and have four white feet, and he'll let no one ride him but me."

Grandmother and granddaughter looked at each other and smiled.

"Tell me some more about when you were little like me," said Daisy. "Begin at the beginning, Grandma."

Madam Gordon told how naughty she had been and how she had always been late to meals and school. She told how she had hated to get dressed up and wouldn't learn to sew or play the piano.

After a long time there was a knock at the door. It was Mose with the tea tray.

"I have a guest, Mose," said Madam Gordon. "Get another cup, please."

Daisy looked with alarm at the thin cup and saucer.

"Don't let that funny old cup frighten you," said Grandma. "She's really a very quiet and sensitive old person. She is almost fifty years older than I am. Try being polite to her and touch her gently. You see, she's afraid you'll break her. But I don't think she'll try to get away from you."

Daisy shouted with laughter. Then she took cup and saucer very carefully from Mose's hand. She sat down on a stool beside Madam Gordon and nibbled her cookie.

"Grandma, how did you get over being naughty?" she asked in a little while.

Madam Gordon got up from her chair without answering. She went to her bureau drawer and came back with a small box in her hand. Daisy's heart sank.

"Oh, dear!" she thought. "That's an earring box."

She jumped to her feet as the old lady seated herself. "I have to go, Grandma," she said quickly.

"I had a nice time. I'm glad you told me about you when you were my age, and about Glory."

"I thought you asked me a question, Juliette," said Madam Gordon. "I was just going to answer it." She took the lid off the box and handed it to Daisy. There, on a piece of red velvet, was a gold locket and chain. "Let me show you what's inside the locket."

"Oh! Oh! Oh!" cried Daisy. "Here's a picture of Glory on this side and a picture of you on the other side. Why, you look like me, Grandma!"

"Juliette, that locket was given to me by my father when I was ten," Grandma Gordon said.

"It was my talisman. Do you know what a talisman is?"

"Fairies give them to people sometimes, don't they?" answered Daisy. "They bring people good luck."

"A talisman is more than that," said Madam Gordon. "Mine reminded me of my father and how anxious he was to have me think before I acted. When I wore it, I was less naughty."

"You mean you were always good?"

"No, my dear, but I tried harder not to be bad," said Grandma. "Do you think that if you wore it you might be reminded too?"

Madam Gordon didn't wait for an answer. She

There, on a piece of red velvet, was a gold locket and chain.

fastened the little chain about Daisy's throat and patted her on the shoulder. "There!" she said. "Now we've been serious long enough for today. Will you come to see me again, little Daisy?"

"Why, Grandma Gordon, you called me Daisy! Now I know you like me."

"And how about you?" said Madam Gordon.

Daisy suddenly gave the old lady a bear hug and ran out of the room. But she came right back. "Grandma, would it be all right to wish on my talisman too?" she asked shyly.

"For a horse, maybe?" asked Grandma. "It might be a good idea."

Chapter 11

Etowah Cliffs at Last

Before long there was a new baby in the family —another little girl, named Mabel. Daisy made a very fine paper doll for her and hung it on the gate.

"Nellie and Daisy are old enough to go to Etowah by themselves this year," Mamma said, after school was over. "I don't like to take such a tiny baby away from home, so the rest of us will stay in Savannah."

Even Nellie was excited about this. It meant that they would go alone on the coach to the little town of Cartersville, Georgia. Aunt Eliza would meet them there.

Three weeks later when Daisy got out of the coach she invited all the other passengers to come and see her in Savannah. "We have lots of big bedrooms," she called to them. "Mamma and Papa would like to have you too."

Aunt Eliza heard her and smiled. Nellie and Daisy piled their bags into her donkey cart. The three were soon on their way down the seven miles of red clay road to the farm.

"I'm sure you know just what you're going to do here, Nellie. But do you, Daisy?" asked Aunt Eliza.

"I'm going to help on the magazine," Daisy answered promptly.

"That's fine, but don't make up your mind too soon. There are many different things to do, and eighteen cousins of all ages to do them with." Aunt Eliza laughed.

After supper that evening Daisy wandered from group to group of young people. She wanted to hear what they were all saying.

"Me for horseback riding and picnics," said one.

"I'm going to swim across the river and back," said another.

"We're going to play hotel in the old schoolhouse in the woods," said a younger girl. "We can use the goat cart and the donkey cart to take our guests back and forth, can't we, Robert?"

"I'm going to make little clay figures for Christmas presents," said another cousin.

"Say, who's going to work on the magazine?" called Caroline Stiles.

Daisy didn't feel enough at home yet to speak up.

"Gee, aren't any of you just going to *play?*" said a tall boy. "Don't you remember the grand games we had over in the woods last year?"

"How about the campfires and the stories?" said another.

Daisy's head was in a whirl. She meant to stay awake for a while and talk to Nellie but they were both too sleepy. The next thing she knew, a bell was ringing. It was time to get up.

After breakfast everyone had chores to do. The tasks and the names of the children who were to do them were written down on a piece of paper posted in the front hall. No one could choose a chore, but the tasks changed hands each week. After this everyone was free for the day, except at mealtime.

Daisy followed Caroline Stiles out of the dining room and told her that she wanted to work on the *Malbone Bouquet*.

"Wonderful!" said Cousin Caroline. "That makes seven on the staff. You meet us here after your chores are done and we'll all walk over to Malbone House together. That's where we work on the magazine."

Much of the work for the magazine was done on a long wooden table under the trees outside Uncle Robert Stiles' comfortable red-brick house. Because she was the only newcomer, Daisy had to sit with her back to the river.

"We each chose a flower for a pen name," said Caroline. "We use these to sign our pieces. I'm 'Clover,' Calla is 'Lily,' Louise is 'Camelia,' Anna is 'Yellow jasmine.' Margaret has already picked 'Daisy.' I guess you'll have to choose another flower."

"I'm 'Rinkaspernum,'" added Harry Elliott.

This crazy name made Daisy laugh. "I'll be a 'Shrub,'" she said. "We're both so sweet."

Everyone laughed.

Each person who worked for the magazine was called a scribe. They carried small notebooks and pencils wherever they went.

"Now who can draw?" asked Caroline. "And who can make up poems? Nellie told us last year that you were awfully good, Shrub. Are you?"

"I'm wonderful!" said Daisy, tossing her head and laughing.

"I'm just the sweetest little Shrub
That ever you did see.
Look close beneath the dark green leaves,
And there you'll find dear me."

The "Flowers" clapped.

"Now the first issue for this summer must be extra good," Clover said seriously. "Each of us must contribute a picture, a poem, a story and some news. We must have them done by July 15 because the *Malbone Bouquet* will be passed out on the first of August."

"What do we do first?" asked Shrub.

"We *think,*" said Rinkaspernum. "I think best when I'm swimming. Goodbye. See you when my wonderful contributions are ready."

"That's just like him," Lily said.

"But he writes the most exciting stories of all of us," said Clover. "His news is usually on the first page too."

"Can we write wherever we like?" asked Shrub.

"Of course—just so everything is ready on the fifteenth," said Clover. "Most of us like to write and draw here. It's more fun. Now here's paper, and we get two pencils apiece. Let's start."

The other flowers seemed to have something to write at once. Shrub scribbled some words but they made no sense. She looked up into the trees and across the fields. Not an idea entered her head. But soon she found herself drawing a picture of a man picking cotton in the field beyond the house.

"Herbert looks just like a woman in your picture, Shrub," said Clover in a little while. "Hold it up for the others to see. You'll have to do better than that."

Shrub was angry. All the pictures she had ever

drawn had been praised. She jumped to her feet. Her eyes flashed.

"Sit down, Shrub," Clover said quietly. "You don't have to help on the *Bouquet,* you know, but if you do, you have to let me decide what's good. I'm the editor."

Daisy was about to crumple up the picture and throw it at Clover when her talisman swung against the table. Suddenly she seemed to hear Grandma's voice, saying, "When I had my talisman it often helped me to think before I acted." Shrub sat down and began to erase the lower part of her picture.

The others looked at one another over her bent head. They didn't know what had happened to make her change her mind so quickly, but they respected her for controlling her quick temper.

The days at Etowah flew by like none that Shrub had ever known. Her notebook was soon almost filled with jottings. She asked for another.

"Let's see what you have," said Clover. "Maybe it isn't all important. Mine is only a quarter full."

Daisy held onto her talisman this time. She didn't know what she'd do if the editor turned down everything she had written, but she wouldn't get mad.

"Say, this is good," said Clover in a few minutes.

Shrub sat down and began to erase the lower part
of her picture.

"Listen, everybody. Look at the picture too. When
did you do this, Shrub?"

"One day when I went to Cartersville with Aunt
Eliza and we took Cousin Buddie with us. I pretended I was Nannie," said Shrub. "The last part of
the poem is—well, it's kind of strange, but—"

"The picture is better, but the poem's not bad,"
said Clover.

"Read it Shrub," said the others.

Little Buddie
by Shrub

Little Nannie and her brother
Walked upon the street together.
Little Buddie was so sweet,
Everybody he did meet
Said to him, "You look so neat!"
Then made answer little Buddie,
"Huddie, huddie, huddie, huddie!"

And he said it with such grace
That they kissed him in the face!
Then a gentleman passed by,
And when Buddie he did spy,
One bright tear dropped from his eye.
"You are like the boy I lost
In the time of snow and frost."
Then, in an assuring study, answered Buddie,
"Huddie! Huddie!"

"That's good enough to go in the August number," said Clover.

Daisy didn't spend all her time on the magazine. She loved the games in the woods. She could imagine that she was really Eleanor Lytle when the "Indians" stole her one afternoon. She demanded that they call her Little-Ship-Under-Full-Sail, and then she told them the story.

"Shrub ought to be in our next play," said Margaret Stiles. "Would you like to, Shrub?"

"Could I be a princess and live in a tower? And could a prince with golden hair and blue eyes come and rescue me?" she asked at once.

"Why don't you write the play?" said Harry Elliott. "I'll be the giant and Robert could be the prince if you like."

So Daisy tried her hand at a play. This was fun too. She helped with the scenery, but she didn't help with the costumes because she couldn't sew.

When the play was performed the tower fell over on the prince and knocked off his blond wig made of shavings. The audience roared, and the poor princess herself couldn't help laughing.

Finally it came time to go home. It had been nearly three months since Daisy and Nellie left Savannah. Daisy carried copies of three issues of the magazine to her father. She had several things in each.

"I just might be a newspaperwoman when I'm grown," Daisy said.

"Well, for goodness' sake!" Nellie cried in disgust. "At one time or another she has said she's going to be a doctor, a missionary, a painter, a sailor, and a sculptor. And now this! I'm glad I know what I really want to do. I want to get married."

"Oh, I'm going to do that too," said Daisy. "I'll have a wedding with ten bridesmaids, and dozens of candles, and everyone will be dressed in white, and. . . ."

"Your husband will be a prince with golden hair and blue eyes, and you'll live in a castle across the sea," teased Nellie.

"That's right," Daisy said shyly. "But you forgot my dozens of children and my stables full of horses."

"You'd better get one horse first."

"I'm still wishing awfully hard for one," said Daisy.

Chapter 12

Happy Christmas Everybody

On the night before Christmas, the Gordon house was beautiful with candlelight and sweet with the perfume of pine branches.

The six young Gordons waited on the stairs for the grandfather clock to strike seven. Two-year-old Mabel sat by Alice. Daisy held baby Arthur on her lap. It was his first Christmas.

Grandma Gordon came sedately down the steps. Mamma and Papa and Nurse followed her. At the same time Liza Hendry and Mose came in from the kitchen.

The clock began to strike. Papa opened the big double doors and the family trooped into the Christmas room. They gathered about a lovely tree covered with dozens of tiny lighted candles.

Papa gave the signal and Mamma began to play

"Silent Night." The children sang the carol. After that, they sat down on the floor. Papa read the Christmas story from the Bible to them, and then it was time for the presents.

Daisy was soon jumping up and down over the fine box of oil paints which Mamma had ordered from New York. The children gave her a palette, brushes, an easel, and stacks of paper.

She was very happy, too, because everyone liked the presents she gave them. She had made most of them herself. There were paper dolls for Alice, a little address book for Nellie, bookmarks for Willy, yarn balls for the babies, and pictures for Papa and Mamma.

Grandma was the last to open hers. When she did, Daisy was very proud, because both Grandma and Papa said that the little clay statue of Glory was really good.

"Even the front legs are right, Daisy child," said Grandma.

"Now the young ones just better get upstairs," said Nurse. "Pretty soon we're going to have plenty of company and dancing and eating and singing. Just think that Miss Eleanor and Miss Daisy are going to stay down with the grownups."

"We'd better see if our hair looks nice and we're spick and span," Nellie said to Daisy. "David is bringing his roommate from school and Randy is bringing his."

The two hurried upstairs together. Daisy looked very solemn for Christmas Eve.

"What did Papa and Grandma give you?" Nellie asked.

"Nothing," said Daisy.

"Oh, they must have. Grandma gave me that beau-ti-ful trunk and two evening dresses and an evening coat, and Papa and Mamma gave me a ring," said Nellie. "You didn't look carefully enough."

"I don't think I'll come downstairs," Daisy said quietly. "I'll watch with the children. Then I'll read a little."

"Silly," said Nellie. "Well, suit yourself. I'm going now."

"Daisy, Daisy, where are you?" shouted Willy. "Come quick. St. Nicholas is here. He wants to see you right away."

The two older girls looked at each other and laughed. This made Willy angry. "All right, you'll be sorry, Juliette Gordon!"

"I didn't mean to tease, Willy," said Daisy. "I'm coming."

"He's out here in the back garden," said Willy.

"You can tell me what St. Nick says," Nellie called.

Daisy followed the little boy through the

decorated house and out the back door. Several people stood there with lanterns in their hands. She blinked. She couldn't believe her eyes.

There before her was a small black horse with four white feet.

"Now, aren't you glad you came?" Willy shouted. "I knew it all the time, and I didn't tell, did I, Daisy?"

"Well, my child," said Grandma's voice from the darkness, "did you think we had forgotten you?"

"Did you have to wait too long, Daisy Dee? We couldn't very well bring Fire into the parlor, could we?" said Papa.

A card on the saddle said: "Merry Christmas from Grandma and Papa."

"Oh! Oh! I just can't think of anything to say," Daisy cried. "It's the most wonderful Christmas present anybody ever had in all the world."

Daisy soon had her treasure bedded down. But Mose wouldn't let her stay and talk to Fire. "You're to go right up to the dancing," he said firmly. "Scoot!"

Daisy had a different idea. She tiptoed up the back stairs and hung over the banister for a few minutes watching the girls and boys. Then she skipped into her room and went to bed.

"I must get to sleep quick," she thought. "To-

A card on the saddle said: "Merry Christmas from
Grandma and Papa."

morrow I'll be riding Fire. Oh, I'm so happy!"

The next morning Christmas firecrackers woke everyone except Daisy. She was already in the stable currying her horse. When she heard the noise she raced out to the gate.

"Come on over," she shouted to Randy, David, and their guests. "You've got to see my horse! Don't bring those shootin' crackers. Fire is highspirited."

The boys shot off several giant crackers just outside the stable. Fire wasn't happy when they all came to his stall.

"We'd better get out of here before he kicks us," said David.

"Where were you last evening, Miss Daisy?" asked Randy's guest.

"Out here in the stable with Fire. Why?"

"I like to dance with pretty girls," said Warrick Evans. "That's why. I'm sure you dance beautifully."

"No, I'm awful." Daisy giggled. "I fall over my partner's feet."

The boys soon left. Captain Gordon came down to give the new member of the family a pat. He said that there could be no ride that day because of the parade of the Fantastiques, men who marched through the streets of Savannah on Christmas Day in masks and costumes.

They dressed as characters from history and

storybooks and plays. There were clowns, and a little red devil who ran through the crowds of onlookers, pinching people and throwing firecrackers among them.

"Oh, Papa, couldn't we dress up in our Halloween costumes and go with them for just a little while?" Daisy and Willy begged together.

Captain Gordon shook his head. Daisy had known what his answer would be.

All day, though she was having a grand time, she was thinking of Fire and of her ride the next morning.

Just before she went to bed she ran into Madam Gordon's room. "Happy, happy Christmas all over again, Grandma!" she said. "And thank you a million, trillion times for my Fire."

Chapter 13

Magic Slippers

Daisy climbed quickly up into the Think Tree with a letter in her hand. The postman had just handed it to her. It was from Randy—the first letter she had ever received from a boy away at boarding school.

"Now I'll have a letter to carry in my pocket, just like the big girls," she thought happily. "I'll answer it at once. Then he'll write again soon."

She ripped open the envelope and began to read. "I'll be home next Saturday. You can be my partner for the first dancing-school party if you like. I've already asked two other girls who couldn't come, and I have to take someone. Randy."

Daisy read it over twice and her eyes flashed. "I do mind, and I won't go with him," she said as she climbed down from the tree. "I'll answer him this minute and I hope he can't find anyone else. It would serve him right."

Her answer was ready by the time the postman reached the house on his return trip. She was back in her room tearing Randy's letter into tiny pieces when Mrs. Gordon came in.

"Randy asked me to be his partner for the dancing-class party," Daisy said. "I won't. He asked two other girls before me."

"But, Daisy, child, you and Randy are best friends," said Mrs. Gordon. "He counts on you to help him out. We'd better talk about this before you decide."

"I decided myself and I gave my answer to the postman," said Daisy. "Anyhow, I'm not going to that party. In the class the teacher always has to make boys dance with me. A dancing party would be awful."

Before Mrs. Gordon could answer, Daisy ran down the stairs and out of the house toward the stable. She was soon in Fire's stall.

"Move over, Fire, I have to curry you hard," she sobbed.

Fire's coat was already shining from his early-morning rubdown, but he didn't mind another.

"I'm not pretty, Fire," she said. "I have an ugly pointed nose and straight black hair and I'm skinny and I stumble when I dance. Just the same,

Randy wasn't fair, was he?"

The horse whinnied and nibbled at her shoulder. Daisy threw her arms around his neck and rubbed her face against it. "Oh, you beautiful! You understand, don't you?" she said slowly. "Don't worry, honey. I'm not mad any more. I guess if I were Randy I wouldn't ask me first either. But it . . . it would be kind of nice to be pretty and to get *first* invitations."

In a short time Daisy was singing as she carried her paints out into the garden. She heard the grownups' voices in the sitting room but paid no attention to what they were saying until she heard her own name. Then she listened closely.

"I wonder why Randy didn't ask Daisy first?" Grandma was saying. "She is far prettier than most of the girls. The idea of her declining his invitation without asking us!"

"I say, 'Good for her!'" Captain Gordon laughed. "Let the child alone, Mother. She won't be thirteen until the thirty-first of October. She has plenty of time to go to parties. One of these days she'll outshine all the other girls. She's going to be beautiful, and interesting and charming as well."

"That's probably so, William," Daisy's mother said. "But just now she feels awkward and left out of things."

"A nice birthday party would be just the thing for her," said Grandma. "More of a grown-up party than usual. We might even have a little dancing in the parlor."

"You're right, Mother Gordon," said Mamma. "We can ask all of our friends and hers too. I'll get her a new dress in New York, a party dress with frills."

"Our Daisy certainly won't like that," said Papa. "Give her a taffy pull and let the guests bob for apples. It isn't every girl who is lucky enough to be born on Halloween."

Before the grownups could go on with their plans, Daisy rushed in. She was excited and smiling.

"I heard what you said. I guess I ought to have called that I was listening, but I didn't." Her words tumbled over one another. "I'd like the dancing part of the party, Mamma. And, please, can the dress be pink with little ruffles? And, Grandma, I'd like to wear earrings if you'll fix my ears."

"What's all this about?" Mr. Gordon said. "I thought that you didn't like parties."

Daisy blushed. She hid her head against his shoulder. "I-I always thought I was *ugly*," she whispered. "If I'm not, then maybe if I had a party dress, as Mamma said, and . . . and . . . earrings . . . and things, maybe the boys would ask me to dance."

"Now you see, William," said Grandma with a smile. "We could make it a fancydress party, and you might be a princess, Daisy. Would you like that?"

"Yes, oh, yes!" said Daisy. "May I, Mamma?"

Mamma said, "We'll see. Dear me, the thirty-first is only a month away! I'll have to order your dress at once."

"Now, Daisy, no time like the present," said Grandma. "We'll fix your ears right away. Come along."

Suddenly all the doubts Daisy had ever had about earrings, frilly dresses and dancing parties came to her mind. She gulped. "Maybe . . . maybe . . . I'll change my mind—and have the apple bobbing after all, Mamma," she said slowly.

"Now, Daisy, child, don't be scared. That's not like you," said Grandma.

"I'm not scared of having my ears pierced," said Daisy. She frowned. "I just don't think I really want to be ladylike."

Finally the evening of the party arrived. The garden looked like fairyland. Bright Japanese lanterns were strung from tree to tree. Mose stood at the front door, in a new purple uniform and white gloves. Some of his friends were already tuning up their banjos and fiddles in the parlor. Upstairs Nurse and the little children were hanging over the banister, watching.

Daisy was looking at herself in a long mirror. She turned around slowly. Her pink dress was so soft that it looked like a cloud. The long full skirt was made of dozens of tiny ruffles. She wore a small golden crown on her head. She held a nosegay of roses in one hand and her pink mask in the other.

"Why, I look . . . sort of . . . almost *pretty,*" she whispered. Her cheeks grew pink. "But what'll I do if nobody asks me to dance?"

She leaned close to look at the dainty coral earrings. Suddenly in the mirror she saw a goblin standing just behind her.

"Close your eyes, Princess," it said. "This is a special night. Do you feel the magic in the air, Your Highness? Hold out first one foot and then the other. And then don't look until you hear music."

Daisy giggled as she closed her eyes. Papa's voice sounded so funny through his mask. She felt her black slippers being taken off her feet. Why, Papa was putting different slippers on her!

"There, Princess," said the goblin's voice. "Have lots of fun, and don't forget your fairy tale."

Daisy heard quick footsteps cross the room. Then she heard music from downstairs. She opened her eyes and looked at her feet.

"Golden slippers!" she gasped. "Just like the ones in my fairy story. My goodness! If I am kind to people while I wear them, their magic will bring me luck, happiness and fun. That's what the story said. That's what Papa meant."

Daisy whirled around and started for the door. She felt scared and excited and happy all at once. Was this how grown-up ladies felt?

"Nurse, please put on my mask," she said. "My fingers won't work."

"Miss Daisy, honey, you look *beautiful*," said Nurse, as she helped her.

"Oh!" breathed little Mabel. "May I touch your dress, Daisy?"

Daisy smiled at her little sister. She pulled her dress up to show her slippers. "Look, honey, Daisy has golden slippers like the Princess in the story."

Then she saw guests were coming in the front door. There was a group of her school friends at the bottom of the steps. Daisy pretended she was a real princess. She held her head high and walked slowly down the stairs.

"Look, here comes a princess," said a familiar voice at the bottom of the steps. "May I have the first dance, Your Highness?"

Daisy giggled at the Indian who bowed to her. It was Randy, she knew.

"Hurry up and make up your mind. Here comes a clown and I think he's going to ask you too." The Indian grunted.

"I can't dance with anyone for a long time, honest I can't," said Daisy. "Grandma says I have to stand in line with her and Mamma and Papa until all the grownups have come.

"I'm sorry I wrote that letter," Daisy said in a low voice. "I was just mad."

"Oh, never mind," said Randy. "I guess I *was* stupid about the way I invited you. I'll come back for you later."

Daisy smiled and went over to join Grandma in line.

Only the thought of her magic slippers kept Daisy sweet-tempered during the next half hour. She wanted to be with her own friends. Then the Indian came back and Grandma said Daisy could go.

But Daisy saw Mrs. Nelson, Madam Gordon's special friend, coming toward her.

"Duck," Randy whispered.

"I can't," Daisy whispered back. "She's old. I must talk to her."

But finally she managed to excuse herself and

Some of her friends spent most of the time dancing.

could join the children. Then, for her, the party really began.

All the T.A.C.'s were there and most of the older pupils of the school. They soon had their masks off. Now they didn't look like witches, goblins, clowns,

Indians, kings, queens, and princesses. Some of them spent most of the time dancing, but not Daisy. It was much more fun to play the guessing games Mamma had planned.

At last Randy dragged her back to the parlor. They galloped about to the music. And then

Warrick Evans asked her to dance.

"Wouldn't you rather go out and join the pecan hunt? The one who finds the most gets a prize," Daisy said breathlessly.

"No, I want to dance first," said Randy's friend.

"I'll probably stumble. I told you I would at Christmas," said Daisy.

"No, you won't," said Warrick. "Come on."

Suddenly Daisy found that she didn't stumble at all. Warrick guided her carefully about the room just as he had the other girls.

"Why, you dance beautifully," he said. "You like it too, don't you?"

"Well, yes," said Daisy. "It's fun, dancing with you. Let's do it again." But just then the music changed to Dixie. "Oh, it's time for the birthday cake and peach ice cream!" Daisy cried.

Warrick pulled her hand through his bent arm. "May I have the pleasure, Miss Juliette?" he said.

Suddenly Daisy felt very grownup. She remembered to say, "Thank you, Mr. Evans." She even let him lead her sedately out into the garden where the supper table was set. There she blew out her thirteen candles and began to cut her cake.

The T.A.C.'s were the last to go. They sat on the steps and talked and tried to finish up all the ice cream.

"Daisy, I have a secret to tell you," said Randy. "I haven't told a person, not even my family. I'm going to be a lawyer. Judge Perkins says I can read law in his office when I'm through school."

"Why, Randy, that's scrumbunctious," said Daisy. "I'm sure you'll be a very good lawyer."

"It's nice to know a girl who won't tell secrets," he said quietly. "Do you know something? You're different tonight. You aren't such a tomboy— you're awful pretty, too."

Daisy didn't answer. She had just spilled her ice cream in her surprise. Imagine Randy talking to her this way!

"Say, would you like to come to the Christmas dancing-school party with me?" Randy said, just before he left.

"If you ask me first, I might," Daisy teased.

It took her a long time to get to sleep that night. She wanted to think about everything that had happened. She touched her magic slippers under her pillow.

"Maybe it wasn't really the golden slippers that made everything so nice," she thought. "Maybe . . . maybe it will be more fun to grow up than I thought it would be."

Chapter 14

Juliette's Gift

Twelve years had passed. It was November 21, 1886 — Daisy Gordon's wedding day. In Daisy's room Mrs. Gordon and Nurse were helping the bride put on her wedding gown and veil.

"Miss Daisy, honey, you are the beautifulest lady that ever got herself married," Nurse said proudly. "I spoke my mind to Mr. William Mackay Low about taking mighty fine care of my baby."

"You didn't, Nurse!" said Daisy. "My goodness, I wonder what Willy thought of that?"

She and Mrs. Gordon laughed. Mr. William Mackay Low was the young Englishman to whom Juliette Magill Gordon was to be married in half an hour.

Daisy handed her mother a diamond pin. "Mamma, will you please put on my present from

Willy? That should bring me luck—because this is your own wedding anniversary and you and Papa have been so happy.

Mrs. Gordon looked admiringly at the pin before she fastened it carefully in the lace at Daisy's throat. "It is very beautiful, dear. And to think that Willy designed it himself, and selected the diamonds too. He's a very clever young man, Daisy. He knows so much."

"He's a very wonderful young man," said Daisy. "The most wonderful I ever met. Oh, Mamma, wasn't it nice of him to give each of my six bridesmaids a pin, too? And to have them shaped like daisies, with the date 1886 engraved on the stems?"

"Seems you are kind of fond of that young man, honey," said Nurse. "You are a mighty handsome couple. Him so yellow-haired and blue-eyed and tall like an oak tree. You just little and pretty with your black hair and those big eyes of yours."

"Daisy, it's time to leave for the church," Mr. Gordon called from the hall. "May I come in?"

"Of course, Papa." Daisy hurried to open the door. "Do you like my dress? And does my bouquet look just right?"

Mr. Gordon had sudden tears in his eyes when he saw Daisy in her wedding dress. "I should give you another pair of golden slippers," he said quickly, to keep from being solemn. "You look exactly like the little girl who was scared to go downstairs on her thirteenth birthday."

"Oh, Papa, I do not!" Daisy laughed. "I'm grown up. Even Mose says I am. Anyhow, let me whisper in your ear. *I have those same golden slippers in my suitcase.* I still like to pretend there's magic in them."

Mr. Gordon patted her shoulder.

Daisy's white chiffon gown had a high neck and long sleeves. *Her* lace veil, which Grandma Gordon had worn at *her* wedding, was as long as her train. She carried a simple bouquet of lilies of the valley.

"All right?" she asked her father.

"Lovely, dear. Now here is something for you to wear that is blue," he said. "You know, 'Something old . . .'"

"'Something old, something new, something borrowed, something blue,'" Daisy chanted. "Papa! My talisman, with a blue stone set in it! Oh, Papa, I do love you so much. You have the nicest ideas!"

"And here is the handkerchief I carried thirty years ago today," said Mrs. Gordon, with a smile.

"Now, Daisy, my dear, don't look sad. This isn't a funeral, you know. It's a happy, happy occasion."

Daisy winked back her tears. Then she gave them each a hug. "Time to go. I was only crying because everything is so wonderful and I'm so happy."

Nurse picked up Daisy's train and they started out. When they reached the head of the stairs she shook her finger at the bride. "Mind, now, you don't slide down that banister, honey."

Everyone laughed. Nurse had cheered them all up but herself. She couldn't bear to think of her favorite child leaving Savannah to live across the ocean in England.

Old Christ Church in Savannah was overflowing with Daisy's friends. Guests had come from as far away as New York, Chicago and St. Louis. There were old and young from the surrounding countryside.

It was a white wedding, which Daisy had always wanted. Tall white candles glowed among lovely bunches of white roses in the church. Soon the wedding march began. Everyone stood up, to turn and look at the bride. There was a second when they all wondered if this beautiful young woman could be the excitable, lively, harumscarum Daisy Gordon they all knew.

Those in the front pew saw the smile which the young couple gave each other at the altar. And those in the back pews could hear both Juliette's and William's responses.

"Listen to that child speak up," whispered Mose to Liza Hendry. "And he did too. That's real lucky, Liza."

After the wedding the Gordon house was filled with guests. All these friends came to wish the couple happiness. Everyone wanted a piece of wedding cake. It was the finest cake Liza Hendry had ever baked.

The wedding guests passed down the reception line. "Oh, Daisy, how we shall miss you," said one.

Juliette laughed. "Not for a while. William's mother lived in Savannah, you know. His father has given us their beautiful old house on Lafayette Square for a wedding present. We'll always have a home here."

"But won't Mr. Low have to return to England?"

"Yes, we'll go next summer, and I can hardly wait! When I was a little girl I used to dream of living in a castle. Willy knows about one in Scotland that we may go to. Won't that be exciting? But we'll have lots of good times in Savannah first and we'll come back here often," Juliette promised.

Twenty years later Juliette Low was living in her castle in Scotland. But she was no longer as happy as the bride who had been married in Savannah. William Low had died. Now Juliette felt that everything was over for her. She tried to

It was the finest cake Liza Hendry had ever baked.

do the same things that she and Willy had done. But she didn't really enjoy the riding, the hunting, the parties. Her friends said she needed a new interest.

What could it be? Juliette didn't know. She tried painting, because she had always liked that, then sculpture. Perhaps that would help fill her life.

One morning she was working on a small statue of a child. Her fingers were deft and quick in modeling. One of her weekend guests, Sir Robert Baden-Powell, came up and praised her work.

"Oh, it's good enough," Mrs. Low said carelessly. "But my heart isn't in it. How I wish there was something new to do."

Sir Robert smiled. "New things are not always easy and pleasant," he said. "I've discovered that in my work to establish the Boy Scouts."

Juliette turned abruptly to him. "Oh, I've heard about your program, Sir Robert. People are calling it a great game for boys. I hoped to learn more about it when you came this weekend. Won't you please tell me? From the beginning—and don't leave out a single thing."

"You are really interested?"

"Very much—and I wish I could be of some help. I love young people, and this sounds like such a splendid thing for boys." Juliette had been covering her work. Now she gave Sir Robert all her attention.

He told her how the idea had come to him when he was in the army, stationed in South Africa. The new soldiers he had to train knew little about nature or outdoor living. They could not stand the hard life. He had to teach them how to be self-reliant and resourceful. He described the games and activities he had planned for them. He explained how this program was even better for boys. It would build physical fitness and character. It would promote friendship, understanding, love of the outdoors.

As he talked he had no doubt of Juliette Low's interest. Her eyes were bright. Her cheeks grew pink.

Suddenly she interrupted. "But why should all of this be only for boys? When I was a child in Georgia my cousins and I all loved our summers in the country the girls as much as the boys. Girls ought to have this same program of Scouting, too, and I'll help them get it. I'll start a troop of the little Scotch lassies who live in this valley!"

"My sister Agnes felt the same way," said Sir Robert with a smile. "She has already organized the sisters of our boys' troops."

"That's splendid! She's laid the foundation. Now

"Girls ought to have this same program of Scouting, too, and I'll help them get it. I'll start a troop of the little Scotch lassies who live in this valley!"

I'll help her," Mrs. Low declared. "I'll begin this very afternoon. Girls will love these activities." She gazed out across the moors, busy with plans. Her eyes were sparkling as they hadn't since Willy died.

"It's a marvelous idea. Why didn't someone think of it when I was little? The T.A.C.'s would have loved it," she went on excitedly. "We can start troops in the villages, towns, and even in London. We'll have—" A new thought struck her. "Why, Sir

Robert, I could take Scouting across the ocean to America! I'm just the one to do it. I know eight no, nine little girls in Savannah who would adore it. I can hardly wait to hear what my niece Daisy Gordon and Randy's daughter, Page Anderson, will say about it. It's a wonderful opportunity for girls!

"What fun they can have! Why, Girl Scouts can . . ."

"We call them Girl Guides, Mrs. Low," said Sir Robert quietly. "It's not easy work, my dear lady. It takes hours and days of planning and a great deal of money. Many girls' parents object strongly to Scouting. They fear it will make tomboys of their daughters."

Juliette Low laughed. "Fine! That makes me like Girl Scouting better than ever. I love a good fight, Sir Robert. And now I have the time to devote to it. But you're right. I'll learn as much as I can here, before I sail for America. It will not be easy there, either. But one troop of girls in Savannah will start Scouting. Soon there'll be another, then three or four—then troops in my whole state of Georgia, then in every state from the Atlantic to the Pacific, from the Great Lakes to the Gulf."

"My dear Mrs. Low, you amaze me. I believe

your American energy and enthusiasm could overcome any difficulties."

"I hope so," said Juliette Low seriously. "It will be a tremendous challenge . . . but I'll bring a wonderful gift to the girls of my country. Everything else I've done will seem small beside this. Why, Sir Robert, who knows what my work may lead to? Someday in my United States of America there may be hundreds . . . thousands—even a million Girl Scouts!"

END

What Happened Next?

• Juliette Low founded the first "Girl Guide" troops in Savannah, Georgia in 1912 when she was 51 years old. The name was changed to "Girl Scouts" the next year.

• Eighteen girls joined the first Girl Guide troops. By the early 21st century, the Girl Scouts® had extended membership to millions of girls world-wide.

• Juliette Low died in 1927.

For more information about Juliette Low, visit the Patria Press website at www.patriapress.com

OR

Visit the Girl Scouts® of the USA website at http://www.gsusa.org/

Fun Facts About Juliette Low*

• Juliette loved fishing. In fact, she would often go out fishing with the men after a formal dinner, still wearing her evening dress.

• Juliette enjoyed telling stories, especially ghost stories around the campfire!

• An accomplished artist and sculptor, Juliette also once forged a set of iron gates.

• Juliette Low's birthplace in Savannah, Georgia is open to the public.

For more information about Juliette Low,
visit the Patria Press website at www.patriapress.com

*Thank you to Laura Humphrey, Lone Star Girl Scout® Council, for permission to use these facts.

About the Author

HELEN BOYD HIGGINS was born in Columbus, Indiana in 1892. She was the author of numerous children's books, including *Alec Hamilton, The Little Lion, Stephen Foster, Boy Minstrel, Noah Webster, Boy of Words, Walter Reed, Boy Who Wanted to Know,* and *Old Trails and New.* Mrs. Higgins also penned *Our Burt Lake Story.*

She was dedicated to enlightening the lives of children by presenting them with histories of significant men and women of our country.

Submitted by William Higgins